O9-AHS-536

Meghan Rose
Takes the Cake

written by
Lori Z. Scott

illustrated by
Stacy Curtis

Standard®
PUBLISHING
Cincinnati, Ohio

Published by Standard Publishing, Cincinnati, Ohio
www.standardpub.com

Text Copyright © 2010 by Lori Z. Scott
Illustrations Copyright © 2010 by Stacy Curtis

All rights reserved. #25445. Manufactured in Grand Rapids,
MI, USA, August 2011. No part of this book may be
reproduced in any form, except for brief quotations in reviews,
without the written permission of the publisher.

Printed in: United States of America
Project editor: Diane Stortz

ISBN 978-0-7847-2930-4

Library of Congress Cataloging-in-Publication Data

Scott, Lori Z., 1965-
  Meghan Rose takes the cake / written by Lori Z. Scott ;
illustrated by Stacy Curtis.
      p. cm.
  Summary: As Meghan Rose works hard to help her class
win a Penny War at school, she prays for God's help in
remembering that the point is to raise money for a food pantry,
not to beat mean Sophie's class. Includes discussion questions
and activities.
  ISBN 978-0-7847-2930-4 (perfect bound)
 [1. Moneymaking projects--Fiction. 2. Contests--Fiction. 3.
Schools--Fiction. 4. Generosity--Fiction. 5. Christian life--
Fiction.] I. Curtis, Stacy, ill. II. Title.
  PZ7.S42675Mft 2010
  [Fic]--dc22

                                    2010029292

16 15 14 13 12 11   2 3 4 5 6 7 8 9 10

Contents

Penny War

"Happy Monday, Park Elementary! Welcome to school on this fine day!" The voice of our principal, Mr. Nelson, crackled over the loudspeaker. Boy, he sounded yappy-happy.

Of course, that's probably because he had not just said goodbye to his grandpa after a fun weekend visit. Which is what I, Meghan Rose Thompson, had to do. I bet if Mr. Nelson had to say goodbye to his grandpa, he'd be all droopy-droop slouchy. Just like me.

Mr. Nelson babbled about the school lunch menu and playground rules. I stuck my fingers into my pocket and pulled out an old brown penny and a shiny new penny. My Grandpa Wright gave them to me before he left when I wouldn't let go of him. (Because who wants to let go of their grandpa, especially when he smells like a deck of cards?)

Grandpa told me to keep the pennies in my pocket every day. The old penny would remind me of him whenever I missed him (like RIGHT NOW). Plus whenever I saw it, I could pray for him. The new penny would remind me that he is praying for me too.

"Wowie, Grandpa," I said. "That makes cents!" Then we laughed at my great joke.

I called them my prayer pennies. I

would keep them forever so I could think about Grandpa and his deck-of-cards smell whenever I wanted to. Even when I was slouched all droopy-droop in my chair at school.

Mr. Nelson talked on. "Thanksgiving is only a few weeks away. Our school is holding a Penny War contest to raise money for the local food pantry."

Penny War? Contest? My ears perked up!

"We raised four hundred dollars during last year's Penny War," Mr. Nelson said. "This year we hope to raise six hundred dollars. As a reward, the classroom that earns the most points wins a cake party from Just Desserts Bakery. Each student in the winning classroom also will receive a coupon for a free cookie at Just Desserts."

My heart went *BUMP-bump*. Kids all started talking at once. My first-grade teacher, Mrs. Arnold, dropped her pen. That's because Just Desserts Bakery has the best yummy-tummy sweets ever.

Just Desserts Bakery also sells the lip-smackingest coffee cake (which doesn't actually have any coffee in it), monkey bread (which doesn't actually have any monkeys in it), and Italian bread (which doesn't actually have any Italians in it).

Mr. Nelson continued. "Your goal is to collect the most pennies in your classroom bucket as possible. Each penny earns your class a positive point. Rolls of pennies count as double points. All paper money and other coins besides pennies earn negative points. So try to put pennies in your own classroom bucket and all other money—

quarters, dimes, nickels, and dollars—in other classroom buckets. The class with the most points after lunch next Monday will be the winner!

"Each class must keep a running count of points and update their daily totals on a graph that will be near the office. That way everyone can check the score each day.

"And there's more," Mr. Nelson said. "Just Desserts Bakery is also running a slogan contest as part of our Penny War. All students can submit a slogan about helping those in need. Just Desserts will add twenty dollars—that's two thousand pennies—to the winning student's classroom total. Good luck."

Isn't it funny how my sad, missing-Grandpa mood switched to a zip-zap, *ka-ching!* money-making mood just like that? I put my prayer pennies back in my pocket.

Meanwhile, Mrs. Arnold tossed a handful of pennies into our Penny War bucket. Then she shook it to get our attention. She's that kind of teacher.

It worked, of course.

"For the Penny War, I need a team of students to count coins," Mrs. Arnold said. "They will also take the money and our total points down to the office each day. This is a great chance to practice addition, subtraction, and counting skills in a real-life setting."

That sounded like something right out of a teacher's manual. I raised my hand. "Excuse me," I said. "Some people call that extra math work."

"I call it extra fun," Mrs. Arnold said. "Because the team gets to work with two of our fourth-grade reading buddies. Michael Rimsky and Lissie Cook have volunteered to help you with the counting and graphing."

My heart beat faster. Michael was MY reading buddy. And he was a real hoot. (That's what Grandpa calls someone who is funny. I don't actually think owls are funny. But I like how *hoot* sounds.)

Michael probably was a whiz with money. A money man. A penny packer. A nickel-and-dime kind of guy. Just thinking about him made me bounce in my seat like a hiccup. Which made my prayer pennies jingle-jangle in my pocket.

Mrs. Arnold raised an eyebrow at me. I think she knew I was hooked.

I wasn't the only one. Soon Mrs. Arnold had a team together . . . with me at the top of the list!

Booger Balls and Butterflies

My friend Lynette smoothed a napkin down in front of her lunchbox. "We can win the Penny War. My dad throws his pocket change into a jar at home. He's got tons of coins."

"I have a drawer full of plastic pizza-box tables and a dead beetle," my friend Kayla said. "That's worth something."

Lynette frowned. "Pizza tables don't earn points."

"But you never know when they'll come in handy," Kayla said. "Everyone loves plastic pizza tables."

"That's because they keep the pizza-box lid from sagging onto the cheese," Lynette said.

"Oh," Kayla said. "I thought they were prizes. It did seem a little boring to always get the same thing. Burger Palace mixes it up when you get their kid meals. I once got the Bouncy-Boingy Burger Booger Ball. It was green and sticky and slimy, and when I threw it—"

I interrupted. "Never mind. You may think that's cool, but it's-snot."

No one laughed at my joke. Which also was-snot cool. So I changed the subject. "I hope we win the Penny War."

"You won't," someone behind me said.

"My class will win. I promise."

I turned. Sophie. From Mrs. Killeen's first-grade class. Her red shirt, red and black plaid skirt, black tights, and black shoes all matched perfectly. But her eyes looked like hard brown marbles. Her lips made a long flat line. Her arms were folded. Sophie always looked and sounded like she was bossing someone around.

Lynette jumped up. Her face turned red enough to match Sophie's shirt.

Kayla waved. "Hi, Sophie! Do you want any plastic pizza tables?"

First, Sophie glared at Lynette. Then she put on a sugary smile and turned to Kayla. "No, you can keep them. You never know when they'll come in handy."

Kayla looked like she might burst. "That's just what I said." She elbowed me.

Hard. "Didn't I say that?"

I ignored her. "What makes you so sure you'll win?" I asked Sophie.

"My mom has more pocket change than anyone else in the school," Sophie said.

"So?"

The corner of Sophie's lip curled in a mean way. "So . . . I want to win." She looked right at Lynette. "And I can't think of anyone, nope, not *anyone*, who can stand in my way. My class will win. I promise."

Sophie turned quickly and left.

I looked at Lynette. "Why was Sophie glaring at you?"

"We don't get along very well," Lynette said. "She's in my dance class. We both wanted to be the butterfly princess at the dance recital. I'm the best dancer, but she got the part."

"Why?"

Lynette lowered her voice. "Her mom made a big fuss about it," she said. "And Sophie threatened to quit."

"Never mind," I said. "It's no big deal."

"Not wanting pizza tables, now *that's* a big deal," Kayla said.

Lynette made fists with her hands. "It is a big deal. I should have been the butterfly princess, not Sophie."

Kayla popped a chip into her mouth. "I didn't even know butterflies had princesses," she said, crunching away. "I wonder if dragonflies kidnap them and lock them in castle towers."

"Sure," I said. "And king butterflies called monarchs ride on horseflies to rescue them. And they live happily ever after with houseflies as servants. Plus outfield flies take care of their garden."

Kayla gasped. "Really?"

"Of course not!" Lynette snapped.

I tapped my chin. "Do you think Sophie will talk her mom into giving her enough money to win the contest?"

Lynette nodded.

"Then that takes all the fun out of it," I said.

We sat in glum silence. Not complete glum silence, though, because Kayla kept eating chips—*crunch, crunch, crunch*. And ninety other first graders kept jabbering and slurping and burping. And the lunch ladies laughed over some spilled milk, which is just wrong if you ask me.

Finally, I said, "What if we can earn more money than Sophie can get from her mom? What if we come up with a plan to earn more pennies than . . . uh . . ."

"Than a roomful of ducks?" Kayla said.

"Exactly," I said. "More pennies than a room full of ducks." Whatever that meant.

"What do you have in mind?" Lynette asked.

I gave her my slyest smile. "Nothing—yet."

Marshmallow Meghan

After school, Ryan plopped down next to me on the bus. "So it's you, me, Lynette, Kayla, and Adam on the penny-counting team?"

"Yes."

"I'm hunting for pennies under vending machines," Ryan said. The bus pulled out of the school parking lot. "Once my brother found a quarter under one."

"Fine," I said. "But how many vending

machines are there around here? We need high-paying jobs."

"I could take my cat for a walk."

"What kind of job is that? Cats walk themselves. How about feeding the cat? That makes more sense."

"I do that anyway. My mom won't pay me for something I already do."

"True," I said. We thought about that in silence. Except, again, it wasn't really silence because the bus chugged and squeaked down the road. And the windows rattled. And kids talked in loud voices. Plus the radio played full blast. And I might have heard a goat.

"We could hold a garage sale!" I said.

"Nah. Too much work."

"We could sell lemonade."

Nodding, Ryan gave me a big smile.

Then his smile fell off. "It's nearly Thanksgiving," he said. "People drink lemonade in the summer. No one would buy it from us now. How about selling cookies?"

"We have Oreos. But I licked all the frosting out of the centers," I said. "Do you have any?"

"No." Ryan made a face. "Dad's dieting."

"Rats. How about . . . soup!"

Ryan rolled his eyes. "Yes, we have soup. But we're NOT selling soup!"

"I'm just trying to think of things parents keep around the house," I said with a pout. "Peanut butter, pickles, and coffee . . . ketchup, macaroni, and—marshmallows! Mom brought marshmallows home from the store last week!"

Ryan snapped his fingers. "I hid a bag from Dad. I forgot about them until now."

I shrugged. "That's OK. Marshmallows last forever if the bag hasn't been opened. We can sell them for five pennies apiece."

"There must be at least a MILLION marshmallows in a bag. We could make a bunch of money." Ryan punched the air. "This war is on!"

As soon as we got off the bus, Ryan went home to get his red wagon. He brought it over to my house to be our marshmallow stand.

I carried out the chairs from my play-table set for us to sit on. Mom helped me make a big sign that said, "Marshmallows 5¢ each."

Several cars stopped right away. Not everyone had pennies, but Ryan pointed out we could put the silver coins in other classroom buckets. We sold half a bag in twenty minutes. Plus we each ate one. Except Ryan had seven. Or eight, possibly.

But not enough cars were stopping. Then *BLAM*, I had an idea to change that. "We need a mascot. Burger Palace has someone dressed up like a cow. He points cars to the restaurant."

"People don't eat there because of the cow," Ryan said.

"How do you know? And quit eating our marshmallows."

Ryan popped another marshmallow into his mouth. I glared at him. He swallowed it fast.

"Do you have a costume?" he asked.

"I have something better," I said. "Toilet paper."

Soon I was wrapped from head to waist in toilet paper, holding a new sign that said, "We need pennies!" and waving at people in their cars.

A shiny lemon-yellow PT Cruiser pulled over to the curb.

Behind the wheel sat a lady so fancy that the color of her lips and nails actually

Marsh- mallows 5¢ each

matched the cell phone she was holding to her ear.

Dark red.

Then the passenger-side window went down, and guess who poked her head out?

Sophie.

She laughed. It was not a nice laugh.

Obviously, Sophie's mom was too busy talking on her phone to notice Sophie's not-niceness.

"What are you supposed to be?" Sophie called.

"I'm Marshmallow Meghan," I said. "I'm selling marshmallows for five pennies apiece. And let me tell you, I'm raking in the cash."

"I don't need to dress up like food to raise money," Sophie said. "Mommy gave me ten dollars' worth of pennies just for being so cute."

My mouth fell open. I stood like a toilet-paper-covered-with-one-end-blowing-in-the-wind statue.

Then Sophie gave me that sugary smile again. "See you at school."

Her window whizzed shut.

"Aaarggghhh!" I said as the car drove off.

I whipped around just in time to see Ryan stuff another marshmallow into his mouth. His face went pink and he shrugged. "Want one?"

"Aaarggghhh!" I said again.

Are You Sure?

Tink, *tink*, *tink*. The last three pennies we earned dropped into the bucket. Wowie. A lot of pennies filled that bucket! But a lot of silver coins did too.

"Tell Lynette I put those quarters in your bucket just for her," Sophie called from across the hall. Then she flounced into her classroom.

Flouncing is *not* one of my favorite ways to walk. It's annoying.

Flouncing is only interesting if the flouncer is dressed up like a friendly, frolicking, floppy-footed frog. But even then it's still annoying.

I worried about Sophie's flouncing all morning. During math I whispered to Lynette, "Are you ready to count the money?"

"Sure," Lynette whispered back.

I watched the minute hand drag around the clock. Why is it that when you're waiting for something to happen, time moves as slow as the last bit of ketchup dripping out of the bottle?

I leaned forward again. "Are you sure you're sure?"

"I'm sure I'm sure."

I tapped her shoulder. "How can you be sure you're sure?"

She shrugged me off. "Because I'm sure."

"Are you sure?"

Lynette might have growled at me then, but I'm not sure.

Next thing I knew, Mrs. Arnold was standing beside me. "Do you have a question, Meghan?"

"No," I said. "But Mrs. Arnold, could you please pick up the pace?"

Mrs. Arnold raised one eyebrow. Then she smiled like a hungry shark.

Let me tell you, time not only flew after that, it flounced! I have never completed three worksheets so fast in my life. I'm sure of that.

When lunch recess finally began, we dumped the Penny War bucket out on the reading table. Mrs. Arnold went to get our reading-buddy helpers.

Ryan didn't want to wait. "Adam and I will start counting the pennies."

"When Lissie gets here," Lynette said, "we'll count the silver coins and get the final total."

"Michael will help me graph the number," I said.

Kayla bounced up and down. "And I'll roll the pennies."

"What?" Lynette said.

"Roll the pennies," Kayla repeated. "Mr. Nelson said rolled pennies count double."

We all looked at each other. Lynette said, "I think he meant something like a tube full of pennies."

I bit my lip. Then I said, "Are you sure?"

Lynette huffed at me.

"Well, I'm rolling pennies," Kayla said. She turned a penny on its side, held it with one finger, and flicked it with another. It spun around like a top.

"That's spinning, not rolling," I said. "Let me try."

Using a book, I set up a ramp. At the top, I put a penny on its edge and let go. It rolled down the slope like a kid on a sled.

"Wowie," I said. "That's fun."

And it was fun. Everyone but Lynette joined in. By the time Mrs. Arnold came back with our reading buddies, we were all laughing. And squealing. And pennies were rolling all over the floor.

Mrs. Arnold folded her arms. Her toe went *tap-tap*.

We stopped laughing. And squealing. And rolling.

"What's going on?" Mrs. Arnold said.

You could have heard a penny drop. I cleared my throat. "We started counting and

. . . I guess we got . . . on a roll. But that's a good thing since rolled pennies count double. Right?"

Then Lissie and Michael burst out with loud *HA-HA-HA-HAs*. (Lissie even snorted.)

Mrs. Arnold covered her face with her hands. Her whole body shook. It took me a minute to figure out she was laughing too. Finally she said, "A roll of pennies, not roll your pennies. Banks roll up pennies in a paper tube to make them easier to count."

"Told you," Lynette whispered with a told-you-so smile. "I knew I was right about the penny rolls. In fact, I was *sure.*"

We finished counting before recess was over. Mrs. Arnold asked, "How did we do?"

"You had three hundred and thirty-seven pennies for positive points and three dollars and fifteen cents for negative points," Lissie said. "So your class earned twenty-two points."

That seemed to make Mrs. Arnold happy. Lynette scooped up the change. Then Michael and I went down to the office to turn in the money and graph our points.

For the first time, I felt like we had a chance to win the Penny War contest. In fact, I was *sure* we did.

Thief!

Mom bought me another package of marshmallows, and I sold them after school on Tuesday. So on Wednesday you could hear pennies jingling in my backpack when I got on the bus.

Ryan's backpack jingled with pennies too. Believe it or not, he earned seventy-five cents walking his cat.

We stopped at the office to check the Penny War graph. Lots of kids crowded around it, including Sophie.

I pushed to the front for a better look.

Bad news. Our class wasn't winning.

Good news. Mrs. Robison's fourth-grade class was in the lead. If I rooted for any class but mine, it would be our fourth-grade reading buddies' class.

Sophie stomped her foot. "This can't be right," she snarled.

I lost control of my mouth then.

"I bet those fourth graders did chores to raise money," I said. "What did you do, Sophie? Oh, I remember. Your mom paid you for being cute." I paused. "On second thought, maybe being cute *was* a chore."

Sophie scowled at me. "We'll see how cute things look, Marshmallow Meghan." Then she stomped off toward the fourth-grade hall.

"I don't trust her," I said to Ryan. "Come on. Let's follow."

Sophie pulled a small puffy bag out of her backpack. She held up the bag and called to kids in the hall. Excited fourth graders fished around in their pockets and handed over—

"Pennies!" Ryan cried. "Everyone is giving her their pennies."

"Marshmallows!" I cried. "Sophie is selling marshmallows. She stole my idea."

"At least she's earning the money this time."

"Not really," I said. "She's taking money that was already going into a bucket. That's like taking money out of one bucket and putting it into hers!"

"That's not the worst part," Ryan said. "Look."

My eyes bulged like a frog's. Sophie even stole my mascot idea. And the marshmallow mascot all wrapped up in toilet paper was KAYLA!

Kayla saw us and raced over. "Hi! I'm a marshmallow." She had fastened an entire roll of toilet paper in between her piggy tails.

"Kayla!" I cried. "Why are you helping Sophie? She doesn't even like you."

"Yes she does. She let me dress up like a marshmallow."

"That doesn't mean she likes you."

"Don't be silly," Kayla said. "Everyone likes marshmallows."

I grabbed Kayla's hand and dragged her away. "Dress up for our team instead."

"OK," Kayla said. "But can I be something else?"

"I thought you said you like being a marshmallow."

"I do," Kayla said, tugging the roll off her head. "But I need to use the bathroom."

Bad news. When we graphed our points after lunch, Sophie's classroom had jumped into first place.

Mrs. Robinson's class visited us for reading buddies that afternoon. I decided Michael should know how I felt about the marshmallow mess. When we sat down, I pointed my finger at him. "You blew the lead!"

Michael pushed up his round glasses. "What?"

"I saw lots of fourth graders buying marshmallows from Sophie. Now her class is winning."

Michael grinned and pushed my hand away. "Don't worry. Everyone always gangs up on the classroom in the lead. It's better to wait until the top rooms do each other in. Then, at the end, you sneak up from behind with a load of coins."

"Except spending all your coins on marshmallows helps the team you want to beat," I said. "Plus you lose the money you're supposed to sneak up from behind with."

"Just remember why we're collecting money in the first place," Michael said.

"To help stock the food pantry." I frowned. "I guess I forgot about that."

"A lot of kids do."

"I still want to win."

Michael nodded. "A lot of kids do. But this contest is about more than winning. It's about helping other people. That's called generosity."

"Giving pennies isn't very generous."

"It is if it's all you've got."

That made me remember a story from the Bible. Some rich people put loads of money into a church offering. They were show-offs, like Sophie. But Jesus saw one woman put in two VERY SMALL coins. And she wasn't showing off. She gave because she loved God, plain and simple.

Jesus saw what she did, and it made him happy. He said she gave more than anyone else because those two coins were all she had.

The story reminded me about my prayer pennies. I touched my pocket. Still safe. I wasn't going to waste them on some contest, no matter how much I wanted to win.

But I decided maybe I should spend less time worrying about Sophie and more time praying for a generous attitude.

"I still don't think fourth graders should buy any more marshmallows from Sophie," I said.

Michael shrugged. "You can't stop them."

I grinned. "Watch me."

Pizza Tables

I met Kayla in the hall after I got off the bus Thursday morning.

Mom had bought me another bag of marshmallows. I pulled them out of my backpack and handed them to Kayla. "You know what to do?"

Kayla took the bag and nodded. "I stand in the hallway near Sophie. Every time she tries to sell a marshmallow, I give one away for free."

"Right," I said. "Kids won't buy something they can get for free. Then their money will go in their own buckets. It will keep the contest fair."

"Sophie will be mad."

I shrugged. "Sophie needs to find an honest way to make money."

"I don't like mad people. Why don't you do it?"

"Because you look great with that toilet paper in your hair."

Kayla patted her head. "I do look nice," she agreed. "Maybe Sophie won't be mad if I give her my pizza tables."

"She doesn't want your pizza tables."

"Everyone wants pizza tables."

"If that's true," I said, "why do you keep trying to give them away?"

Kayla shrugged. "I collect them. But I

don't know what to do with them."

An idea popped *BLAM* into my head. My heart went *BUMP-bump*.

"I want your pizza tables!" I said.

"Why? Are you mad at me?"

"No. I'll explain later. I have more figuring to do."

"It figures," Kayla said.

"Just take care of the marshmallows."

At lunchtime Kayla reported to the counting team. "It worked!" she said. "I kept Sophie from selling marshmallows."

Lynette clapped. "Way to go, Kayla! You take the cake."

"Goody," said Kayla. "What cake?"

"Not a real cake," Lynette said. "It's something my dad said after I danced really well at my recital. When someone says you take the cake, that means you're the best at something."

"So it's like a fancy way of saying WOWIE," I said.

"Wowie for what?" Kayla asked.

"Wowie for stopping Sophie from tricking the fourth graders into putting their pennies into her classroom bucket," I said.

"It was your idea," Kayla said.

"I know. And I have another idea. Just listen to this! I thought about Kayla's pizza tables and other useless stuff we all might have lying around the house."

Kayla choked. "Useless?"

"I have a few pizza tables at home too," I said. "Plus some old wrapped candy and plastic Easter eggs."

"Me too," Lynette said.

Ryan and Adam nodded.

I took a big breath. "So bring that stuff

and come over to my house on Saturday morning. We are going to create some fine works of art to sell. In the meantime, do some chores for pay. You know, water your fish. Lick stamps. Clip toenails. Got it?"

"Got it," Lynette said.

"Yippee!" Kayla's eyes sparkled. "Didn't I tell you? You never know when pizza tables will come in handy."

Slogan

After our spelling test on Friday, Mrs. Arnold said, "If you recall, Just Desserts Bakery is running a slogan contest along with the Penny War."

Kayla raised her hand. "What's a slogan?"

Mrs. Arnold loves a what-or-why kind of question. She gets that hungry-shark look in her eyes when someone asks a question like "What makes a rainbow?" or "Why does the moon change shape?" She especially loves a what-*and*-why question like "What is the difference between jelly and jam, and why does it go so well with peanut butter?"

Mrs. Arnold said, "A slogan is a catchy motto or a jingle. It promotes an idea. For example, what comes to mind when I say hamburger kid's meal?"

I shouted, "Burger Palace!"

Then the whole class chanted, "Beefy burgers on a bun with mustard-pickles-ketchup and fun, fun, fun!"

"The Burger Palace slogan sticks in your mind," Mrs. Arnold said. "It connects their food with having fun. You'll be doing something like that for Just Desserts, connecting their food with the idea of helping the hungry. Plus, I suspect the bakery hopes the contest will get the attention of a local newspaper or radio or TV station. That could get them free advertising, which is always good for business."

"So how do we make a slogan?" Kayla asked.

"Simple," Mrs. Arnold said. "Think about the idea behind the Penny War. Then write about it."

I chewed on my pencil and thought.

First I thought about what Michael said. The real goal of the Penny War was to help other people. But there was nothing catchy or jingly there. I needed something more to work with.

Time for a what-and-why question. Except I didn't ask Mrs. Arnold. I asked God. Because God doesn't get that hungry-shark look when you talk to him.

"Dear God," I whispered. "I've spent a

lot of time collecting pennies. But I haven't thought much about the people who will get the money and how it will help them. What good will pennies do? They're only worth a cent apiece, and they're so . . . *common.* And why use us kids to collect them?"

All this thinking about pennies reminded me of Grandpa. So I quickly added, "And P.S., I am not talking about giving *my* prayer pennies. Those are different."

I squeezed my eyes shut and waited. And while I waited, I remembered buying food with Mom at the grocery store. I wondered how much food each bucket could buy if everyone at school gave in a generous way. I bet Jesus would be happy with us, just like he was happy with the woman in the Bible story.

Then I remembered how hungry I felt

the day I accidentally skipped breakfast. And wow—when lunchtime finally came, I smiled as wide as Texas.

I remembered how when our class worked together, we filled the bucket up zippy-quicky. A bucketful of pennies meant a bucketful of food and a bucketful of Texas-sized smiles.

Then BLAM! An idea popped into my mind. Love is like a penny! If you drop love into your heart bucket, it fills up zippy-quicky with smiles too! Come to think of it, you could drop love like pennies into everyone's heart bucket and fill them up with smiles. It just makes sense—or cents, *ha-ha*—to act that way.

So putting together my common pennies with my friend's common pennies plus the whole school's common pennies could—

would—do a lot.

And why use us kids to collect pennies? Well . . . why not? Just because we're little doesn't mean we can't do big things.

"Meghan."

I opened one eye. Mrs. Arnold stood over my desk. She did not look happy. "You've got a slogan to write."

"Amen," I said. "Wait right there, Mrs. Arnold, because I've got it."

I smoothed out my paper. I wrote one sentence. I handed my paper to Mrs. Arnold.

She glanced at it and smiled. It was not a hungry-shark kind of smile. It looked softer.

"Not bad," she said. "Why don't you find something to do while everyone finishes?"

I pulled out another piece of paper and

drew my pizza-table idea. Because I had a penny-earning plan. One that just might take the cake.

PEAs

On Saturday morning everyone crowded into my room. We dumped pizza tables, candy, and plastic Easter eggs on my bed. Then we all plopped down on the floor.

Except me. I felt too kangaroo bouncy to sit. Plus I was holding something behind my back. Plus Kayla was lying down and kicking like she was making a snow angel, and she took up most of the floor.

"Mom ordered pizza for lunch," I said.

"We can work all day if we have to."

"Yay!" Kayla squealed. "Peat-zzah, peat-zzah, peat-zzah!"

Lynette folded her arms. "This better be good."

"Yeah," said Ryan. "I'm missing Super Cat . . . my favorite cartoon."

"Don't worry," I said, waving my free hand. "I thought of everything. My mom is recording Super Cat for you."

Adam cleared his throat. "So what are we making? And why?"

A what-and-why question. Perfect. I put on a hungry-shark look as toothy as Mrs. Arnold's. "I'll answer the why first. Why are we doing this?"

"So we can beat Sophie's class," Lynette said.

"And win a cake party and cookie

coupons," Kayla said.

"And most important," I said, "so our school can help buy food for the food pantry."

Adam nodded. "But what is the what?"

"The what is THIS," I said. I showed everyone what I had been hiding behind my back. "I turned a pizza table upside down so it could hold this orange plastic Easter egg.

I put candy in the bottom of the egg to make it heavier. That way it won't tip over. Then, with a black marker, I drew ears, eyes, nose, paws, and stripes."

"It's a tiger," said Lynette.

"I call it a PEA—Pizza Egg Animal. What do you think?"

Kayla clapped. "I want a PEA! I want a PEA!"

"I like it," Lynette said.

"I could make a yellow duck," Kayla said. "Wearing a snorkel. Because *duck* and *snorkel* are two of my favorite words."

Ryan laughed. "How about a purple cow? Or a pink elephant!"

Adam grabbed a green egg off the bed. "I'm making an army alligator."

By the time the afternoon ended, we had all our PEAs lined up on my dresser.

"Now we have to sell our PEAs over the weekend," I said. I looked at Lynette. "If we sell them for seventy-five cents each—"

A smile crept across her face. She took a big breath and let it out. "We might make sixty dollars," she whispered.

We all stared at each other with our mouths wide open.

Because, let me tell you, that's a whole lot of pennies.

9

Cash Clash

"Success!" Ryan yelled when I got on the bus Monday morning. He lifted his backpack. "Feel how heavy this is."

"Wowie," I said.

"I sold my PEAs during my brother's basketball game. All except this one." He held up a red Super Cat PEA. "This one's mine."

I grinned. "I sold all of mine at church. To a teacher in the five-year-old Sunday school class. She loved them!"

"I bet no one drops in as many pennies as we do today!" Ryan said. "But be quiet about it. That way, no one will see us coming from behind to take the lead and win."

"Good idea," I said. "I'm ready for a great big two-layer cake. With circus stripes on the bottom part. And blue frosting with pink swirls on the top part."

"Yum!" Ryan said. "And jelly beans around the center."

"Plus candy stars," I said, "and cookie flowers and lollipops sticking out all over the place like cat whiskers. Something so incredibly tummy-yummy, it could only come from Just Desserts."

We both sighed just thinking about it.

On our way to our class, we watched some big kids drop silver coins into every bucket they passed.

Outside one of the kindergarten rooms, a boy ahead of me clutched a cup full of coins to his chest. But his shoelaces were untied. He tripped. The pennies fell with a loud *TING, TING, TING* and rolled all over the floor.

The kid sat up and rubbed his knee. Then he started to cry.

"It's OK," I said. "I'll help you."

I helped him up. We searched for his pennies and snatched them up as fast as we could.

I saw Sophie pick several *somethings* off the floor too. Then she looked around fast before throwing them into her classroom bucket.

I frowned. "Those aren't your pennies, Sophie!"

Sophie shrugged. "What are you talking about?"

I looked her straight in the eye. "This poor boy—"

"Robby," he said.

"This poor Robby dropped his pennies. And instead of giving them back, you took them."

Sophie sniffed. "I did not."

"Yes, you did. You robbed Robby."

"Prove it."

I huffed. I puffed. But I could not prove it.

Sophie smiled like a panther.

Still sniffling, Robby wiped his face on his sleeve.

I patted his back. Then I looked Sophie's direction again and reached into my backpack. "You can have some of my pennies, Robby," I said in a loud voice. "My friends and I brought tons. About sixty dollars' worth."

The smile fell off Sophie's face.

"Yep," I repeated. "Sixty dollars. Six thousand pennies."

So much for keeping quiet about it.

Sophie stomped off toward the office. "I'm getting my mom!"

"Thanks for helping me," Robby said. "You're the nicest first grader."

Robby's words made my heart swell with happy like a sponge full of water. Whether or not my class won, I felt good helping Robby. I felt good knowing I was helping hungry kids with faces I'd never see. And I felt good knowing that I earned the money myself.

As I emptied my backpack into our

bucket, I felt a sharp tap on my shoulder.

There stood Sophie with a mean glint in her eye. "I want to win," she said. "But I want you to lose more than I want to win. And you will lose. I promise."

"It's not about winning," I said. "It's about doing something to help others."

"Whatever," Sophie snapped. Then she dropped three twenty-dollar bills into our bucket. One. At. A. Time. "Twenty. Forty. Sixty dollars. Good thing my mom was in the office so I could help myself to her wallet."

My stomach flopped. Now, just like that, the negative points from Sophie's bills would cancel out all our hard-earned penny points.

As the bell rang, Sophie marched to her room. I sagged against my classroom door.

"We're doomed," I groaned. "And it's all my fault."

Dog Pile

At lunchtime, I chewed on a fingernail and watched the team count.

It took a l-o-n-g time because there was so much money.

Finally, Lissie sighed.

"That doesn't sound good," Ryan said.

"It's not," Lissie said. "You've got a last-place-for-sure total."

My whole body felt numb, like when you go outside on a freezing cold day without a coat. The prayer pennies in my pocket suddenly felt heavy. I hadn't put them in our bucket. And now even if I did, they would not make a difference. We would still lose.

"It's my fault," I said. "I made Sophie mad. I didn't keep our sixty dollars quiet."

I lifted the twenty-dollar bills out of the pile. "She got even."

My friends shifted in their seats. Then Kayla reached out and patted my arm. "You just aren't a quiet girl. That's OK. I'm not a quiet girl either. Especially not if there are ducks or snorkels or pizza tables around."

"But we had fun anyway," Lynette said. "And we helped the food pantry."

I tried to smile, but the smile kept sliding off my face. "I know. But I feel like I let everyone down."

"You did," Kayla said. "But we don't

hold your loud blah-blah-blah mouth against you."

I slouched. "Thanks."

"Come on," Michael said. "Let's go graph the results."

Lynette put an arm around me. "I'll go too. I know how it feels to have Sophie spoil your day."

Ryan stepped up. "I'll come."

"Me too," Adam said.

Lissie shrugged. "I guess we'll all go."

"Yay!" Kayla squealed. "DOG PILE!!"

Somehow Kayla launched herself into the air like a rocket. Lissie and Michael escaped, but the rest of us fell into a giggling, wiggling, get-off-you're-squishing-me heap.

Good friends are like that. They squish all the unhappy out of you.

We were the last class to post results.

Lissie studied the graph. "Look at that. Every class ended with low numbers."

"How did that happen?" I asked.

"Someone probably put silver coins in all the buckets," Lynette said. "Even a few quarters brings the total way down."

I perked up. "Then we still have a chance?"

Lissie shook her head. "No. You're still in last place."

"Who's ahead?" Kayla asked.

"Right now it's hard to tell," Michael said. He squinted at the graph. "The lines are too close. It could be our class—Mrs. Robison. Or Sophie's class—Mrs. Killeen. We'll have to wait and see."

I hate waiting and seeing. It's like getting a present in July and not being able to open it until Christmas. That's why I spent so much time watching the clock, waiting for the announcements at the end of the day.

And that's why I didn't do my work.

And that's why I wasn't surprised when Mrs. Arnold called me up to her desk.

Mrs. Arnold would make a great detective. All she had to do was look at me, and I blurted everything out.

"I'm sorry I didn't finish my work. I can't stop thinking about the Penny War. Part of me feels happy for earning so much money. A lot of people will have food because of that."

Mrs. Arnold opened her mouth, but I went on.

"But another part of me feels sad for losing. And another part of me feels sad about feeling sad because winning wasn't the real goal. Helping others was the goal.

And that's a good thing, so I shouldn't feel sad."

Before Mrs. Arnold could stop me, I kept going.

"The biggest part of me is angry at Sophie for beating us. Mostly because I think Sophie cheated. I can't prove it, but I think she stole pennies from a kindergartner. And also money from her mom. And that's not fair.

"So I'm angry. And angry is not a very nice feeling to hold inside of you. It keeps wanting to burst out. So I'm angry at myself for feeling angry because I'd rather be laughing."

Mrs. Arnold raised an eyebrow.

"So that's why I didn't finish my work," I said.

Looking at my shoes, I handed Mrs.

Arnold my paper.

She took my paper, crumpled it up, and tossed it into the wastebasket. I gasped. I had never, ever, ever seen Mrs. Arnold throw away a worksheet.

I believe that might even be against the rules.

But she got my attention.

She's that kind of teacher.

"The principal wants to see you in the office," she said.

I thought I might faint. Had Mr. Nelson heard about my sixty-dollar mess? I was in big trouble.

Maybe I could explain to him how hard it was for me to keep things shut. Things like tubes of toothpaste, cupboard doors, and my mouth.

"Better get going," Mrs. Arnold said.

Blinking back tears, I stumbled out of the room and down the hall.

Just Desserts

Mr. Nelson was waiting for me.

"Hi, Mr. Nelson," I said in a small voice.

"Take a peek at the classroom totals for the contest, Meghan." He handed me a sheet of paper.

When I read the list, my stomach dropped. First place was Mrs. Killeen's class. Mrs. Robison's class finished a close second.

"Your class raised the most money," Mr.

Nelson said. "How about that!"

I frowned. "We came in last."

"That's because you had more silver coins and dollar bills than pennies," he said. "Even so, well done. Your efforts will feed many people. Doesn't that feel good?"

I thought about it for a minute. And *BLAM*, two things popped into my head. First, I realized that even though it hurt to lose, I also had a good snuggle-up-to-Grandpa kind of feeling in my heart. I guess that when you help others, it's hard to give without getting something right back.

"Yes," I said. Then I grinned a little. "Yes, it really does."

"That's the spirit," Mr. Nelson said.

"But I'm not done, Mr. Nelson," I said. Because the Bible story about the poor woman's offering was the second thing that had popped *BLAM* into my head. Taking a big breath, I reached into my pocket. "I'd like you to . . . add these pennies to the total." Then I put my prayer pennies into Mr. Nelson's hand.

Mr. Nelson looked puzzled.

"I earned a lot of pennies for the contest," I said. "But it was easy to give them away because the only thing they cost me was time. And I've got loads of time. I also have loads of empty toilet paper rolls, but that's beside the point."

"And what is the point?" Mr. Nelson asked.

"These two pennies are different," I said. "I LOVE these pennies. They are MINE. So it's hard for me to give them away."

"Then why are you?"

I chose my words carefully. "I want to

see if giving makes a difference when the only difference it makes is to you."

"Uh . . ." Mr. Nelson said.

I tried again. "I mean, does giving mean a little more when it costs you a whole lot?"

Mr. Nelson rubbed his chin. He gave me an I-wonder-what-you're-thinking kind of look. "And does it?"

I took another big breath. I missed my pennies. But I also felt . . . right. It was a feeling like I had when I was sore after hiking around the zoo all day. I hurt but I was happy at the same time. And the happy made the pain OK.

"Yes, Mr. Nelson," I said. "I gave those two pennies because it was my way of showing God that I love him, plain and simple. And I think that made God happy. Plus now my heart feels like it is smiling to the balloon-pop stage."

"Hmm," Mr. Nelson said, cocking his head to the side. "Interesting. Now, I asked you here because I want you to deliver the cookie coupons to the winning classroom." He chuckled. "Have a seat while I make the announcement."

A wave of *oh-no* hit me. Deliver the cookie coupons? To Mrs. Killeen's class? Imagine Sophie smirking at me about that!

But before Mr. Nelson could turn on the loudspeaker, a woman rushed into the office.

A fancy woman. With red lips. And red nails.

Sophie's mom.

"I'm sorry to interrupt, Mr. Nelson," she said, breathing hard. "But I was just at the store, ready to buy Sophie a Hula-

Missoula designer purse, when I discovered that the money I had in my wallet is gone! And I remembered having my purse open this morning in the office when I paid the balance for Sophie's lunch account. So I hurried back here, and . . . well, has anyone turned in any money?"

"No, I'm sorry," Mr. Nelson said.

"Sophie took it," I said.

"What?" Sophie's mom gave me the bulgy-eyed look you sometimes see on a water buffalo at the zoo.

So I explained about Robby dropping his pennies. And about Sophie taking some of them. And about me trying to show off. And about Sophie getting mad.

While I talked, Sophie's mom got puffier and puffier, like a marshmallow. With water-buffalo eyes.

Gulp.

I kept going. "Then Sophie said she was getting you. She came back and put sixty dollars in my classroom's bucket."

For a few moments, Mr. Nelson and Sophie's mom just stood there with bulgy eyes and wide-open mouths. (Fish do that in schools too, but that's different.)

Then Sophie's mom turned to Mr. Nelson. "It seems Sophie unknowingly gave away her Hula-Missoula designer purse."

"It's for a good cause," Mr. Nelson said.

She held up a hand. "Don't worry. You can keep the money. But it shouldn't count against this girl's classroom. Somehow that doesn't seem fair."

Mr. Nelson nodded.

"And . . . I will talk with my daughter tonight. About giving . . . and getting."

Then, just as quickly as she came in, she left.

Mr. Nelson looked thoughtful. He picked up the list again. "Let's see. I'll need to adjust the score for Mrs. Arnold's class . . ."

Two seconds later, he whistled. "Boy, this is one of the closest contests we've ever had!"

"DOES THAT MEAN OUR CLASS WON?" I blurted.

"Just be ready to deliver those coupons," Mr. Nelson said.

Which was not actually a very helpful comment.

Then he turned on the loudspeaker.

Meghan Rose Takes the Cake

"Good afternoon, Park Racers. It's time to announce the Penny War winner. First, I want to thank you all for your efforts. We surpassed our goal of six hundred dollars. Congratulations."

While Mr. Nelson talked, a jumble of thoughts went through my head like a dryer full of mismatched socks.

Squeezing my eyes closed, I prayed. "Hi, God. I need your help right now because part of me would rather flush the cookie coupons in the toilet than deliver them to Sophie's class. And I'm pretty sure that's not the right thing to do. Plus it might clog the toilet. So help me be a good loser. Let me remember all the fun we had . . . and how good it feels to help others. Amen."

I felt better after that. Opening my eyes, I listened again.

"Those are the current standings," Mr. Nelson said. "However, don't forget: Just Desserts Bakery will add two thousand pennies to the total of the class with the slogan-contest winner. That might change the lead."

I sat straight up. Maybe Mrs. Robison's class could still win! Holding my breath, I leaned forward to hear better.

"The winning slogan is 'Helping hungry

people just takes COMMON CENTS.' It was submitted by Meghan Thompson."

I fell out of my chair.

"That puts Mrs. Arnold's class ahead of the current leader. So Mrs. Arnold's class is our school winner!"

I opened my mouth, but nothing came out.

A sound came from outside the office, though.

"EEEEEEEEEEEEEEEEEEEEEEE!"

"Kayla?" My voice sounded like a croaking frog.

Kayla burst into the office, followed by the rest of the class. Everyone squished around me. Plus we bounced up and down.

Mrs. Arnold squeezed into the office too. She held up one finger, and the bouncing stopped.

"Well," she said, smoothing her shirt. "I must say, I've never had an entire class run out on me before."

Mr. Nelson laughed. "Meghan, you take the cake! And I guess you won't have to carry these cookie coupons to the winning classroom after all . . . since the winning classroom is right here."

We cheered.

"Thanks," I said, with a smile as wide as Texas. "But just so you know, I asked God to help me. And I would have been glad to do it."

Mrs. Arnold winked at me. "That's very generous of you," she said. "Meghan Rose, you definitely do take the cake!"

And since I had given away something special just like the woman in the Bible, I knew just what she meant.

Chatter Matters

1. Read the whole story of the poor woman and her offering. Look in Luke 21:1–4 in your Bible. Why do you think Jesus noticed what she did? Why do you think a person's attitude in giving makes a difference?

2. Have you ever donated canned goods to a food pantry? If so, how did you feel about it? Why? Read Romans 12:8 and 1 Timothy 6:18. Sometimes we don't have money or food to donate, but God gives us many other ways to help others. What are you good at doing? How can you use that skill to help others? How else you could help others?

3. Read Isaiah 58:7. Why do you think God encourages us to act this way?

4. What's the difference between giving up something you don't want (like clothes you've outgrown) and giving away something dear to you (like a favorite toy)? Do you think God honors both the easy-to-do and the hard-to-do kind of giving? Why or why not? Read 2 Samuel 24:18–24. What do you think about David's answer to the man who wanted to give him his threshing floor?

5. In your own words, tell what you think the word *generous* means. Then give an example of when someone was generous to you and an example of when you were generous to someone else.

Blam! – Great Activity Ideas

1. Bake a cake (or cookies) and throw a "We Can" party. Ask each friend you invite to bring canned food to the party. You can do things like frost and decorate can-shaped cookies, play "Kick the Can," make the penny-collection container described in activity 3, and dance the can-can. After the party, donate the canned food to your local church.

2. Design your own cookie coupon. Use a 3 x 5 index card (or construction paper), crayons (or markers), and stickers. If you'd like, you can bake cookies and then give your friends or family a cookie coupon for them to trade in for a sweet treat.

3. Make a penny-collection container. You'll need an empty container with a lid (shoeboxes, drink-mix canisters, or Parmesan cheese containers work well), permanent markers, glue, scissors, stickers and paper for decoration, and a handy adult. First, ask your handy adult to cut a slot in the lid of your container. The slot should be wide enough to fit coins through. After the slot is cut, put the lid back on. Next, peel the label off the container. Finally, using markers, stickers, paper, or whatever else you have available, decorate the outside of your container. If you like, you can use your container to collect money for a church offering.

4. Make a PEA. You'll need a clean plastic pizza table, a plastic Easter egg, small stones or wrapped candy, and permanent markers. First, put the small stones or candy in the bottom of the egg to give it weight. Next, use markers to draw a face and body on the egg. (If you'd like, you can decorate the egg with other materials too, like pieces of felt and wiggle eyes.) Last, turn the pizza table upside down and set the egg in it.

5. Spin pennies with a friend. See who can spin her penny the longest.

To Mr. Nelson and the staff at
Richmond Elementary—LZS

For Brylee—SC

Lori Z. Scott graduated from Wheaton College
eons ago. She is a second-grade teacher, a wife, the
mother of two busy teenagers, and a writer. Lori has
published over one hundred articles, short stories,
devotions, puzzles, and poems and has contributed
to over a dozen books.

In her spare time Lori loves doodling, reading the
Sunday comics, and making up lame jokes.

You can find out more about Lori and her books
at www.MeghanRoseSeries.com.

Stacy Curtis is a cartoonist, illustrator,
printmaker, and twin who's illustrated over twenty
children's books, including a *New York Times* best
seller. He and his wife, Jann, live in Oak Lawn,
Illinois, and happily share their home with their dog,
Derby.